the stolen soul

THE TRAPPS FAMILY ADVENTURES

the stolen soul

By LAWRENCE E. R. ADAMS

Illustrations by ROBERT G. ADAMS

TRAPPS PUBLISHING

First Printed in 2008
Printed in Canada

THE PUBLISHER:
Trapps Publishing
P.O. Box 212
Irricana, Alberta, Canada T0M 1B0

Library and Archives Canada Cataloguing in Publication

Adams, Lawrence E. R. (Lawrence Edward Roy), 1941-
The stolen soul / by Lawrence E.R. Adams ; illustrations by Robert G. Adams.

(The Trapps family adventures)
Includes index.
ISBN 978-0-9781532-2-9

1. Inuit--Canada--Fiction. 2. Inuit mythology--Fiction. I. Title.
II. Series: Adams,
Lawrence E. R. (Lawrence Edward Roy), 1941- Trapps family adventures.

PS8601.D454S76 2008   C813'.6   C2007-907552-5

Cover: Robert G. Adams
Printing: Friesens Corporation

Disclaimer

All the characters in this book are fictitious, any resemblance to any living or deceased person is merely a coincidence.

For Judy my wife, we have shared our journey through life.

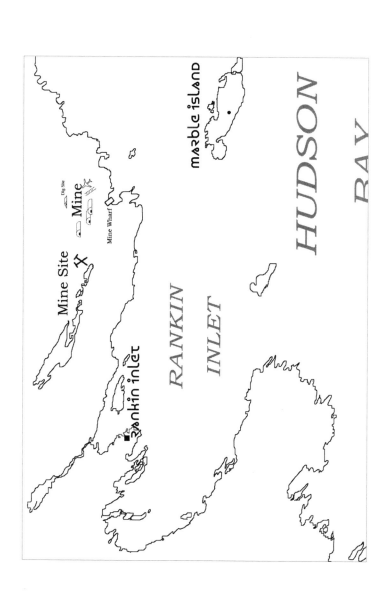

Mine Site

Dig Site
Mine
Mine Wharf

RANKIN INLET

Rankin Inlet

marble island

HUDSON

BAY

CONTENTS

PROLOGUE 9

tasks of a shaman 13

what took you so long 19

road of shadows 29

the dog 37

the river 51

tents of the netherworld 65

the umiak awaits 79

the trip home 81

GLOSSARY 92

PROLOGUE

It wasn't the call of the North that brought the Trapps family to the vast treeless region of Canada's North, known as the Tundra. This trip had nothing to do with the romance that "the call of the North" evoked; this wasn't even going to be a holiday. Numerous hours of backbreaking work would dominate the expedition, or so they thought.

Max Trapps, a world-class archaeologist, has led expeditions to numerous places in the world conducting excavations to uncover the secrets of the past. He has been chosen to conduct an archaeological dig at an ancient Inuit settlement. Workers at the Blue Diamond Mine, approximately thirty kilometres northeast of Rankin Inlet on the west shore of the Hudson Bay in the Northwest Territories, made the discovery while working near their airstrip. For the duration of the dig, the mining company is generously supplying the food and lodgings for the entire Trapps Family.

When Amy and her brothers, Ty and Parker, meet "THE OLD ONE," the secrets and mysteries of the North and the Inuit way of life will be laid bare before them. Nothing the kids might have done before they left their home in Calgary could have prepared them for the adventures they were about to experience. They were entering an environment that few people have ever seen and fewer will ever live in. It is a harsh and unforgiving land that holds untold beauty, mystery, and adventure for those who dare to accept its challenges. The North is home for the Inuit, the only race of humans who are able to live under its conditions without assistance from the outside world. The Inuit's ability to adapt to their environment allows them to reap the bounty of the North. Only the most adventurous and well-equipped explorers have been able to penetrate the Inuit's habitat and live to tell about it.

Amy's curiosity and her thirst for knowledge sometimes gets her into jams that requires the help of her brothers to get out of. She enjoys assisting her father during excavations and likes nothing better than discovering a relic from the past and unlocking its secrets. Ty is twelve, one year younger than Amy, and a gifted athlete. His favorite sport is hockey and if he were allowed, he would play it twenty-four hours a day. Parker, who is one year younger than

Ty, doesn't possess his brother's athletic abilities, but his determination to succeed and to not be outdone by anyone makes him a worthy opponent. He possesses a photographic memory, which has proven to be an asset when his sister gets them involved in one of her many schemes.

After meeting the shaman Kadluk (the adults know him as THE OLD ONE) the kids now have the ability to communicate through their Inuas, a gift that is only bestowed upon shamans. An Inua is the spiritual occupant (spirit helper) that resides in all living and inanimate things.

Kadluk opened a world to the kids that they never knew existed. But when they discovered at the dig the first amulet that had been made by the first shaman, they learned they were protected in a manner that mortal man could only dream about. The amulet gave them protection from anything that would otherwise harm them and allowed them to approach and travel with dangerous animals.

chapter 1

tasks of a shaman

Friday, October 04, 1985

Dear Diary,

     Boy, was I scared when I found myself alone on the Tundra with all those shadows.

Amy

Amy was tired when she got home from the kitchen and did not waste any time getting ready for bed. It had been another long day and the excitement of discovering the amulet had taken its

13

toll; she was ready for a good night's sleep. Amy's head hadn't even hit her pillow when the voice said to her Inua, *"Hurry, the boys are waiting for you! You're going to be late."*

"Late for what? Kadluk is that you?" Amy cried.

"Yes, it is I," said the voice. *"You must hurry."*

"Hurry where? Where are we going?" Amy asked, knowing full well there would be no answer. Sure enough, she was talking to the wind because the voice was now gone. She looked down and could see that she was off the ground. Why are my feet not touching the ground? she thought. She was afraid she was falling, but no, she was just hovering a few feet above the ground. How was this possible? Was she dreaming? What was she doing here? In her mind's eye, visions were starting to take shape; shadowy figures were approaching her and she thought they were asking her questions. Why couldn't she hear what they were saying? Try as she might, she couldn't hear their words. Their mouths were working but no sounds were coming out.

What do they want? Amy wondered. Looking down at herself, Amy realized she was wearing the traditional Inuit clothing: a caribou parka, polar bear pants and sealskin mukluks. This was the same clothing the Shaman Kadluk (THE OLD ONE) always wore. She could also see that the little amulet she had discovered at the dig was sewn to her parka.

Questions rushed through her head: where did I get these clothes? What is happening to me? Slowly it dawned on her that she had somehow entered the spirit world of the shaman.

These figures that kept coming to Amy, what were they? If they were spirits, were they good or bad spirits? Or were they lost souls who were coming to her for help to find their way home?

Two people emerged from the shadows and startled her. "Who are you?" cried Amy. Her skin began to crawl as the creepy feeling of the unknown began taking hold of her. She felt a great sense of relief when she realized it was only Ty and Parker. They were dressed in the same Inuit clothing that she was wearing, and they also had the small amulet sewn to their parkas.

"You scared me, why didn't you answer me?" Amy shouted.

"Jiminy-Willie-Peppers, I'm too scared to speak," whispered Parker.

"What's happening to us? Why are we here?" Ty wanted to know.

"I don't know, Kadluk told me to hurry. He said you were waiting for me, and the next thing I knew I was here with all these scary shadows," Amy told her brothers.

"That's the same thing that happened to us, and since we got here we've been wandering around looking for you," Ty said.

"I think we've entered the spirit world of the shaman, but I don't know why," Amy said.

As shamans, the kids possessed vast powers. The Inuit believe a shaman can shake the earth, make themselves invisible, walk on clouds, have their bodies give off sparks, and fly to the moon or even fly through the universe on a lark.

Amy and her brothers now had the ability to fly off and consult with the deities. They were now part of the Inuit world that linked man with the spirit world. Their people could come to them for help in solving problems that they were unable to deal with themselves. The harmony between the Inuit and their world now rested on the kids' shoulders.

Among the powers that shamans possess is the power to heal. The Inuit believe that spirits are the cause of all illnesses, and so it is understandable that one of the main tasks of a shaman is to cure these illnesses. This could be done in many ways, depending on the sickness. It is believed that evil spirits, breaking tribal customs or the loss of a person's soul, cause most illnesses. Healing took place in a public ceremony. Usually the shaman would call upon the affected person to confess to breaking taboos and then encourage him or her to offer excuses to the offended spirits. The audience was encouraged to take part in the healing process by offering excuses for the sick person. If the shaman determined that the person's soul had wandered off or been stolen, they would send spirit helpers to retrieve it or fly off themselves to retrieve it. In addition to this, shamans are expected to possess practical medical knowledge. Shamans could be called upon to treat burns and major lacerations, amputate gangrenous limbs and set broken bones.

Amy realized that the shaman played a very important role in the lives of the Inuit people and she could see why Shamans were both revered and feared at the same time. Evoking the wrath of a shaman, who held so much power over the lives of so many, could only produce dire consequences for the transgressor.

Still the shadowy figures continued to lurk before Amy and her brothers. What did they want? Who were they?

The figures were scaring Amy. "Who are you? What do you want?" she called out.

"Ty and Parker, can you see those shadowy figures? What do they want? They're giving me the creeps!" Amy told the boys.

"We can see them," the boys answered in unison.

"I don't know what they are or what they want. They just seem to be floating in space," Ty observed.

"Jiminy-Willie-Peppers, they're giving me the creeps too!" cried Parker.

"I wish THE OLD ONE was here, he'd know who or what they are!" Amy flatly stated.

"We can ask him the next time we see him," Parker added.

"Yes, we must remember to ask him when we see him again," Amy said.

chapter ii

what took you so long

"*Come and help me - I've been waiting for you. What took you so long?*" a voice asked through the kids' Inuas.

Frantically, they looked around and realized they were in an Inuit village. An Inuit man lay on a bed of caribou hides and was being attended to by a man who was obviously a shaman, because he was chanting the secret chants of the shaman. It was the shaman's Inua that had spoken to them. Another man sitting behind the shaman held a drum in his left hand and was beating it with the drumstick he held in his right hand. The people of the village sat in a circle around these three. They were calling on the man to confess his sins so that he may be well again.

"Who are you and how did you know we would be coming here?" asked Amy, looking inquiringly at the shaman.

"I am Toolook. I asked my helping spirits to find someone to assist me on my journey to retrieve a stolen soul in the netherworld. The way is long and treacherous, and only the strongest shamans can complete such a dangerous undertaking. My Inua talked to THE OLD ONE and he told me about you. He said you were brave and would help me. You must prepare yourselves for our journey, call your helping spirits to assist you, for we shall need all the help we can get to see us through to the end of our mission."

"But, how did we get here?" Amy wanted to know.

"THE OLD ONE summoned you," Toolook told her.

"Why did he do that?" Amy asked again.

"He told me that if I needed your help he would summon you, and he did," Toolook replied.

"Yes, but how did he get us here?" Amy demanded to know.

"I don't know. How can THE OLD ONE do the things he does? One does not question what THE OLD ONE is capable of doing. He just does what has to be done to maintain harmony in our world." Toolook responded.

"Oh," said Amy, a bewildered look on her face.

While Toolook continued chanting, the kids began to talk to each other.

"What is THE OLD ONE getting us into now? Why isn't he here?" Ty asked.

"Don't get excited Ty," Amy scolded her brother.

"Maybe THE OLD ONE is busy doing something else and he can't be here," offered Parker.

"Yeah I'll just bet!" Ty retorted.

"We have to help - THE OLD ONE said it is our duty as shaman to help the people," Amy reminded her brothers.

"How can we help when we don't know what to do?" Ty sighed, shrugging his shoulders.

"Toolook said he was coming with us. I'm sure he knows what to do and we'll just have to help him," replied Amy.

"I just know this is going to be fun," Parker exclaimed excitedly.

21

"It'll be fun alright," Ty said with a sneer, "what is this netherworld that he said he was going to?"

"I don't know" Amy admitted.

"Kadluk mentioned the netherworld and the never-ending feast once before when we first met him," Parker reminded his sister and brother.

"That's right Kadluk did mention them," Amy said while looking at Ty.

"I'll bet it's a far off place. Do you think we'll be able to fly there?" asked Parker.

"It doesn't sound like a place I want to visit; in fact it sounds rather scary," Ty howled.

*   *   *

"What is wrong and how can we help?" Amy asked Toolook through her Inua.

"This man is very sick. I have tried everything and yet he still does not respond. His friends and relatives have given him their Inyusuq and the evil spirits have not been driven from his body. I have determined that this man's soul has been stolen from him and is being held by his dead relatives' souls in the netherworld. I need your help to retrieve it!" Toolook informed the kids.

22

"*What is Inyusuq?*" Amy wanted to know as she looked inquiringly at Toolook.

"*Yeah, and what's this netherworld you keep talking about?*" Ty demanded to know, with sarcasm in his voice.

"*Inyusuq or personal souls are the powerful forces that reside in all individuals and serve as the source of good health, stamina, willpower and energy. They comprise all the elements that give a person life. The netherworld is where the dead souls go to enjoy the never-ending feast after their journey on earth has ended. Did THE OLD ONE not tell you this?*" Toolook queried, looking suspiciously at the kids.

"*Oh he probably did and I just forgot. This Inyusuq - it drives the evil spirits from the sick person's body when it is given by friends and relatives?*" Amy asked.

"*Of course, that is the only way to get rid of the evil spirits when all else fails,*" replied Toolook. It sounded like doubt was creeping into Toolook's voice as he looked inquisitively at the kids. "*You are the young Kabloonas that THE OLD ONE knows, are you not?*" Toolook inquired.

"*Yes, we are the young white people that know THE OLD ONE, we are his friends. He is showing us the ways of the shaman,*" replied Amy.

23

"Well then you can help me. I have heard that you are strong and wise in the ways of the shaman. I will need your strength and wisdom to complete the journey that I must take without delay," Toolook told the kids.

"Who is that with you and why don't you take him?" Amy asked pointing to the drummer.

"That is my assistant and he does not possess the traits of the shaman and cannot perform the tasks that are required," Toolook answered.

*   *   *

The shaman's assistant sat behind the shaman, methodically beating the drum he was holding, while calling on the shaman's helping spirits to come to his assistance in his time of need. Boom-Boom-Boom went the drum.

"Look at the drum - the handle is carved in the image of a man. What do you suppose that means?" Amy asked, the excitement of a possible discovery clear in her voice.

"I don't know," replied Ty, shrugging his shoulders.

"It's probably carved in the image of a man because we will be seeking a man's stolen soul," Parker remarked as he looked at the drum.

"*I suppose you're going to tell me the images of people hanging from the drum on those leather strips represent the dead souls that have stolen this fellow's soul?*" Amy asked Parker.

"*That would be my guess,*" Parker replied as he peered closely at the drum.

'*There are no feathers hanging from this drum, what does that mean?*" Ty wanted to know.

"*I would say it means we won't be flying on this trip,*" Parker stated.

"*Yeah, you're probably right,*" Amy sighed.

The rhythmic beating of the drum had induced a trance-like state and the Trapps could hear themselves calling to their tutelary spirits, their guardian spirits, to protect them and assist them during their journey to the netherworld. The kids and Toolook called on their ancestors' spirits to stand by them and give them their strength in their time of need during the journey. While the drum continued its rhythmic beat, the relatives of the sick man called on the spirits to assist the kids and Toolook. Before they took their journey, the Trapps and Toolook had to be bound securely to prevent their spirit helpers from flying away. Using the slip knots THE OLD ONE had shown them, they laid on the ground and bound each other until they were immobile, while Toolook's assistant bound Toolook.

25

Once they were bound, the assistant again began to beat the drum while Toolook chanted. The drumbeat continued, Boom-Boom-Boom. The kids joined Toolook chanting the secret chants of the shaman, *"AIIIEEE,"* they chanted.

The villagers shouted words of encouragement and called on Toolook and the kids to be strong during their journey.

As the drum continued to beat, Toolook announced. *"The way is open! I see the Road-of-Shadows that we must travel on to reach the netherworld."*

The villagers all cried, *"go in safety, and be strong!"*

CHAPTER III

ROAD OF SHADOWS

As the drum continued beating, the villagers fell quiet and the Trapps' and Toolook's spirits passed through the drum to start their journey down the Road-of-Shadows to the netherworld.

The shadows were eerie and grotesque and they sprang at the travelers as they wound their way down the Road-of-Shadows. Their spirit helpers told them not to talk to the shadows and save their strength for the tasks ahead. Weaker shamans would be distracted by the shadows and would soon forget why they were there. If this happened, the stolen soul would never be recovered and would be lost forever.

"These look like the same shadows we saw before - do you think they were trying to distract us so we wouldn't help Toolook?" Amy asked Ty and Parker.

"I don't know, but they sure give me the creeps," replied Ty.

"Jiminy-Willie-Peppers, these shadows are spooky and they're scaring the daylights out of me," Parker said while his head swung from side to side and his eyes tried to pierce the darkness for the lurking shadows that were ever present.

"Stay close Parker, they can't hurt you as long as we're all together," Amy told her younger brother. She could sense his uneasiness: when the shadows brushed past them with their hideous laughing and grotesque faces, she felt just as uneasy.

"I think they're harmless and are just trying to distract us and get us off course, don't pay any attention to them," Ty advised the group.

*   *   *

After traveling a long time they came to a house that was built on the north side of the road.

The house appeared to be made out of stone with animal skins for a roof. The front of the house was made from various pieces of wood. The door was crudely made out of odd pieces of boards and planks that were lashed together with strips of animal hide.

"Whose house is that?" Amy asked Toolook through her Inua.

"I think it is the house of the old woman who guards the gateway to the netherworld," replied Toolook.

"Don't you know whose house it is?" Ty cried, as he looked in disbelief at Toolook.

"THE OLD ONE said we would eventually come to the old woman's house I think it must be hers," Toolook said.

"Oh great, we don't even know whose house we're at? Haven't you ever been here before?" Ty shouted at Toolook.

"No, my duties have never required a trip to the netherworld before," Toolook replied.

"I think we're in trouble!" Ty stated, throwing his arms in the air.

"Don't be so pessimistic Ty, THE OLD ONE would not have told Toolook about us if he didn't think we could handle it," Amy said trying to bolster her own courage.

31

"I think Amy's right, THE OLD ONE wouldn't put us in any danger," Parker remarked, the concern plain in his voice.

"You don't call this danger? We don't know where we are or where we're going and we're with someone who has never been here before and doesn't know where he's going. I think you could say we're probably in a little danger, don't you?" Ty stated as he looked from one to the other for an answer.

"Knock on the door Toolook and see if it belongs to the old woman who guards the gateway," said Amy.

Toolook approached the door and gave it three sharp raps with his knuckles. He quickly stepped back and waited for a response. Nothing happened.

"Try again Toolook," Parker insisted rather excitedly, anticipating what might happen next.

Toolook again approached the door and gave it a good loud rap and stepped back.

The door slowly started to move outwards as it was opened from the inside.

From the dark interior emerged a very old woman who barred the doorway. Her wrinkled old face brought to mind the passing of centuries: ever-increasing layers of soil stacked up and bearing down on each other, crushing each other with the ever-increasing pressure. From observing her features, one could not begin to decipher the events that had occurred while she stood her post. Her face was expressionless: nothing could happen that would shock her nor deter her from her post. She had withstood the test of time and would continue to do so. She was small in stature at barely four and a half feet tall. She wore the traditional dress: the caribou parka, polar bear pants and sealskin mukluks. Her hair was long and extended past her shoulders; the black color was long gone and had been replaced with gray. The blue tattoo lines from her bottom lip to her neck were visible and mixed with the wrinkles of time. She looked like a tired old lady who had carried the weight of the world on her shoulders.

"Who are you and what do you want?" hissed the old woman as she glared suspiciously at the intruders.

"Jiminy-Willie-Peppers, she gives me the creeps," stated Parker, backing away from the old woman.

"I am the shaman Toolook and I have come to retrieve a stolen soul and return it to its rightful owner," Toolook advised the old woman.

"Why do you bring Kabloonas to the netherworld?" The old woman wanted to know.

"They are shaman, they are being trained by THE

33

OLD ONE, and have come to assist me on my quest for the stolen soul," replied Toolook.

"Yes, I have heard THE OLD ONE talk of such Kabloonas. Why has THE OLD ONE not come with you, if these are the Kabloonas he is training?" asked the old woman peering intently at Toolook.

"THE OLD ONE is busy with other matters and he said these Kabloonas are strong and brave and would assist me on my quest. One doesn't question the wisdom of THE OLD ONE," Toolook informed the old woman.

"I see," cackled the old woman. *"Time will tell if you are telling the truth; you will be thoroughly tested while you try to complete your journey. You may proceed. If you have not told me the truth it would be best for you to turn around now and leave this place while you are still able to do so."*

With these words, she turned and closed the door. The group stood and stared at the closed door with the old woman's final words ringing in their ears.

"What does she mean when she says we better leave now while we still can?" Amy asked Toolook.

"Yeah, does that mean we have to stay here for ever?" Ty howled while looking at Toolook.

"THE OLD ONE told me if the trip to the

netherworld is not just, then the traveler may have trouble leaving. That's all I know, I don't know how he knows this," Toolook told them.

"Jiminy-Willie-Peppers! I don't like the sounds of this," Parker cried as he looked first at Amy and then at Ty.

"It'll be okay Parker, we'll stick together," Amy assured him.

"I hope you know what you're doing Amy," Ty barked.

"Come we must go quickly, we must not be distracted from our mission, we have no time to lose," Toolook said as he turned and walked toward the Road-of-Shadows.

chapter iv

the dog

On and on the kids and Toolook traveled down the Road-of-Shadows.

"Can you hear that?" Amy asked. *"It sounds like a dog barking."*

"I can hear it and it sounds mad," Parker said as he started to slow his pace.

"Yeah, we can all hear it," grumbled Ty.

"What would a dog be doing on this road?" Amy inquired.

"THE OLD ONE said we had obstacles to overcome before we reached the island - maybe the dog is one of the obstacles," Toolook offered, shrugging his shoulders.

They came upon a vicious dog standing in the middle of the road and barring them from passing. The fangs of the dog were laid bare and spittle flew from its mouth as it snarled and growled and swung its head back and forth trying to bite anything within reach!

"Why is that dog acting so vicious? It's acting like it wants to bite us," shrieked Amy.

"Yeah, we're wearing our amulets, we're supposed to be protected. What's going on?" Ty asked, looking at Toolook.

Toolook shrugged, *"I don't know."*

"Ask the amulets' Inua, Amy!" Parker shouted excitedly.

"Yes, leave it to you to come up with the correct solution to our problem," Amy said to Parker as she smiled at him.

"Why are we not protected from this dog?" Amy asked the amulet's Inua.

"You are not in your world, I have no powers in the netherworld," answered the Inua.

38

"How are we supposed to protect ourselves if you are not protecting us?" Amy wanted to know.

"You have to rely on your shamanistic abilities," the Inua replied.

"What are we going to do now?" Amy cried.

"I say we get out of here while the getting's good, I don't feel like becoming lunch for that dog and he looks mean and hungry enough to eat all of us," retorted Ty.

"We have to retrieve the stolen soul," Toolook reminded the group.

"We've come too far to turn back now," Amy said, looking searchingly at her brothers.

"Ask the dog's Inua why he's so mean and what we have to do to get past him, Amy," Parker howled.

"Why is your dog so mad, is he always like this?" Amy asked the dog's Inua.

"He has been tasked with keeping out those who would cause trouble in the netherworld. He has to be ever vigilant, for he is tested constantly and those who do not belong are soon found out and meet with a cruel fate," came the reply.

"Who would want to cause trouble in the netherworld?" Amy wanted to know.

"Sometimes a Tarrak will disguise itself and try to get into the netherworld to wreak havoc. The dog must protect against this, for the dead souls must have peace *and tranquility to enjoy the never-ending feast that they deserve after their lifelong journey on earth,"* replied the Inua.

"We are on a mission to retrieve a stolen soul and return it to its rightful owner. We have to pass this way for this is the only road. How can we gain a safe passage?" Amy pleaded.

"To the north over that knoll, you will find a small lake where you can catch fish to feed the dog. He will let you pass while he is eating," replied the Inua.

"How can we catch fish when we don't have any fishing tackle with us?" Ty asked to no one in particular.

"You don't need fishing tackle. When you get to the lake you will find there is a sand bar across the lake. The fish must cross this sandbar and when they do, they are exposed and easily caught if one acts quickly," the Inua informed them.

"Is that all we have to do to get past?" asked Amy.

"That is all," came the reply.

"That sounds too easy, there has to be a catch," said Ty.

"Is there a catch?" Amy warily asked the Inua.

"There is no catch, but make sure you catch a large fish or more than one. If you just catch a small one, you will not satisfy his hunger and he will think you tried

to fool him and will get angrier. You will suffer his wrath because he will not let you leave the netherworld if you anger him," advised the Inua.

"Ha! Just as I thought, I knew it sounded too good to be true," bragged Ty, feeling rather proud of himself.

"If all one has to do is catch fish and feed the dog to get past, why don't the Tarrak do this?" asked Amy

"They do when they try to fool the dog, but in their mad blind rage they never remember to get enough fish to ensure their safe passage and are banished to the far side of the island forever," said the Inua.

"Come, we must hurry, we are wasting time," barked Toolook.

"Be careful while fishing, do not slip off the sand bar into the deep water," warned the Inua.

"Why, what's in the deep water?" asked Amy.

"You don't want to know!" came the reply from the dog's Inua.

"Jiminy-Willie-Peppers, I don't like the sounds of this," Parker cried aloud as he looked fearfully at his companions.

"It will be okay Parker, just stay close to me," Amy said as she led the small group towards the knoll.

* * *

Upon reaching the knoll they could see that the sand bar ran the width of the lake. They observed fish spraying water in every direction as they traversed the sand bar.

"This is going to be easy," Ty proclaimed as he viewed the fish.

"It might not be as easy as you think," Parker cautioned as he remembered how slippery other fish had been when they caught them.

"Come on, I'll show you how to catch them," Ty laughed while he ran down the hill and into the water.

"Be careful! Don't go near the edge of the sand bar," Amy warned.

Ty saw a rather large char crossing the sand bar and ran for it. *"I've got one,"* he yelled as he grabbed the char just in front of its tail.

"Way to go Ty!" yelled Parker, reveling in his brother's prowess.

"Oops," muttered Ty. The fish gave a quick wiggle and was gone before Ty had even realized what happened.

"I thought you said you had one!" Amy complained.

"I did have one, but he got away. They're harder to hang onto than I thought," Ty replied.

"When you get close to one, grab him by the tail with your right hand and slip your fingers through his gills with your left hand. If you do this, he won't be able to get away. Otherwise the fish will be too slippery and you won't be able to hold onto him," Toolook advised the kids.

"Why didn't you tell me that sooner, I could've had one by now," Ty complained.

"Never mind, Ty, we'll catch some more," Amy sighed.

The kids and Toolook spent some time running around the sand bar chasing after fish but couldn't seem to catch any.

"We're going to be here all day if this keeps up," observed Parker.

"It's a good thing these clothes are waterproof; in this cold water we'd be frozen to death by now if we were wet," Amy remarked.

"We've got to have a better plan than this running around. We're not getting anywhere and I'm getting tired," wailed Ty.

"Ty's right, stop chasing the little fish and concentrate on the bigger ones because they have the most difficulty in this shallow water. Parker, when the next big one crosses the sand bar, wait until it gets almost all the way across and then run in front of it. When it turns back we should have a chance at catching it," Amy said.

"There's one now," shouted Parker as he pointed to a fine char breaking the surface on its journey across the sand bar.

"Wait!" Amy yelled, *"Okay, now Parker, cut it off!"*

Parker ran as fast as he could and got in front of the fish and it turned thrashing in the water. Amy, Ty and Toolook ran at the startled fish and quickly grabbed for the tail. Ty was the first to make contact and held the tail with both hands as Amy and Toolook secured the head.

"We got him," Ty proudly proclaimed.

"Quickly, let's get him ashore because we still have to catch another one," Amy advised the group.

Now that they had a strategy, the second fish was caught quickly and the group found themselves returning to the Road-of-Shadows to appease the dog and gain safe passage.

As they neared the dog and he caught sight of the fish, he stopped snarling and growling and just looked warily at the group approaching him.

When Amy laid the first fish on the road in front of the dog, he tore into it as though he were starving. *"Keep your hands back, I don't think the dog will distinguish between them and the fish the way that he's eating,"* Amy warned the group.

When Ty laid the other fish before the dog, the dog was so busy consuming the first one that he didn't even acknowledged it.

"Come quickly, we must go, we have no time to lose," pleaded Toolook as he quickly walked past the dog and down the Road-of-Shadows.

"Will this road ever end? It seems like we've been traveling forever and my feet are getting sore," Parker moaned.

"It shouldn't be much farther Parker," Amy said, and then turning to Toolook, she asked. *"How much farther do you think the island is, Toolook?"*

"Not far," Toolook replied.

"What does 'not far' mean?" We've been traveling for hours," Ty whined as he looked at Amy.

Amy shrugged her shoulders as they continued walking down the road in silence, ever wary of the shadows that continued to haunt them.

* * *

"Who's that?" cried Amy as they rounded a curve in the road and a figure appeared from nowhere.

Where nothing had been a few moments before, now stood an old man dressed in traditional

Inuit clothing. He wore the caribou parka with polar bear pants and sealskin mukluks just like THE OLD ONE when they first met him. He said not a word and just stared at them. His frame was bent from the passing of time and a demeanor which suggested his travels would never end. The aging wrinkles that crisscrossed his face told the story of a never-ending struggle with life.

"*Jiminy-Willie-Peppers, I don't like the looks of this,*" Parker said as he looked at the old man.

The group stopped in their tracks and stared at the old man in the middle of the road who was staring back at them.

"*Who are you, and why do you dare travel the Road-of-Shadows?*" yelled the old man.

"*I am Toolook and these are the young Kabloonas who have come to help me recover a stolen soul from the netherworld,*" replied Toolook.

"*What stolen soul? Who said there's a stolen soul here?*" howled the old man.

"*I did. I am Toolook, the shaman, and I am convinced that a sick man's soul has been stolen and is being held by his dead relatives in the netherworld,*" Toolook informed the old man.

"*Who are you?*" Amy asked the old man on the road.

"*I-Am-The-Keeper,*" the old man replied.

46

"*The keeper of what?*" Ty inquired as he looked at the old man.

"*I am the Keeper of the dead souls in the netherworld,*" replied the man on the road.

"*Then you know about the stolen soul?*" Amy asked the Keeper.

"*I know of no stolen soul!*" the Keeper flatly stated.

"*But you must know!*" Parker pleaded.

"*I know of no such soul!*" the Keeper replied again.

"*Could you have made a mistake, Toolook? Are you sure the soul is here?*" Amy questioned Toolook.

"*Yeah, we could be making this trip for nothing. The Keeper sounds pretty sure the soul isn't here. Maybe we should turn back,*" said Ty, looking at each member of the group pleadingly.

"*THE OLD ONE said that if we encountered the Keeper we might have problems with him. THE OLD ONE said the Keeper doesn't like visitors because he only wants the souls who will be staying in the netherworld to travel the Road-Of-Shadows,*" Toolook told the kids.

"*What else did THE OLD ONE tell you that you haven't told us?*" Ty wanted to know.

"*Ty, we're all in this together,*" Amy said to her brother.

"*THE OLD ONE said to tell the Keeper we are not dead souls, we are flesh and blood and will not be staying in the netherworld,*" Toolook advised the kids.

Together, the kids and Toolook spoke: "*stand aside - we are flesh and blood we will not be staying in the netherworld.*"

The Keeper grudgingly stepped aside to let the group pass. If he had the power, he would have made them stay, but he did not possess the power to control souls that had not been sent for him to watch over. The group continued their journey while the Keeper stared after them as they traveled the Road-Of-Shadows.

chapter v

the river

They could hear the roar of the rushing water long before they reached the knoll that lay in front of them. An uneasy feeling crept over the group because they could feel that the river was a killer before they could see it. The first view of the raging river left them spellbound. They felt utter despair as they viewed the river and watched the rolling water kick up its spray to the wind. Far across the river they could see the shoreline of the island that was called the netherworld.

"That island is huge! I can't even see the ends of it!" Parker howled.

"We can't cross that! Look how far away the island is!" exclaimed Ty.

"We have no choice; we have to. See the tents on the island? They are the tents of the souls of the netherworld. That is where we will find the lost soul," cried Toolook.

"How are we going to get across?" Amy asked.

"Because the current is so swift, we'll never be able to wade or swim across. A kayak only holds one person so we'll need an Umiak to transport all of us at once," Parker observed.

"We must find a Umiak, then. Quick, search the shore!" Toolook pleaded.

"From what I understand, an Umiak is kind of hard to paddle and hard to control in rough water. How will we ever be able to navigate one in that raging current?" Ty inquired as he looked at Toolook.

"That depends on who made it - some are better than others. We'll have to see what we can find," Toolook said to Ty.

"Jiminy-Willie-Peppers, I don't like the looks of this," groaned Parker.

"Ty, you and Parker search the shore to the right and Toolook and I will search this way," Amy commanded.

"We can't go very far - look at the cliffs that rise up. They must be 200 feet tall!" exclaimed Ty.

"Well, check the shore up to the cliffs and then come back," Amy ordered.

"If I had my kayak, this current would be nothing to me. On the other hand, a Umiak in this fast current will be like a whale caught in shallow water and it will surely flounder," Toolook mused.

Ty and Parker hadn't walked a hundred yards up the shore before they found an Umiak on the bank of a little backwater.

Ty ran to get Amy and Toolook while Parker stayed with the Umiak.

Toolook's heart sank when he first saw the Umiak. Whoever made the craft, had used caribou antlers for the ribs that were tied to a piece of planking that was used for the keel. No doubt, the planking had been a piece of driftwood at some point in time. The gunwales were made of more bone and secured to the tips of the antlers by strips of sealskin. The walrus hide that was stretched over this framework had seen better days and appeared to be on its last legs. Although Toolook could see no holes in the hide he could tell from years of experience that this craft had seen better days. It wasn't made very well and was almost as round as it was long. Inside the craft were four paddles fashioned from caribou antler with the pan of the antler acting as the paddle. From the looks of the Umiak it could have been here from the dawn of time. He dared not say anything to the young Kabloonas about the poor design and quality of the craft they were about to use.

The group apprehensively boarded their newfound mode of transportation. No one was relishing the thought of taking this craft into the raging waters that lay before them. It would take all of them paddling as fast as they could in order to reach the island without being swept away by the current and lost down stream forever.

"*It's a good thing the young Kabloonas are with me, for surely I will need their strength to paddle this Umiak to the island shore,*" Toolook muttered to himself.

When the group shoved off from the rocky shore, they knew they were in for a wild ride. The current spun them around and around as they furiously paddled and tried to gain headway towards the island.

"*Jiminy-Willie-Peppers, that water is cold!*" yelled a startled Parker as the icy cold spray of water hit him in the face.

"*Faster!*" shouted Amy. "*We must paddle faster.*"

"*Yes faster,*" Ty yelled to no one in particular as he dug his paddle deeper into the raging waters.

The cumbersome craft was not meant for this kind of water and was difficult to maneuver; it tossed to and fro and spun like a top on the crest of the rushing water. The current gave them a ride they would not soon forget: they were completely out of control.

"*I'm getting dizzy from all this rocking and spinning,*" shouted Parker.

"*Hang in there and keep paddling Parker! We must synchronize our paddling! We're getting nowhere this way. All together now: one-two-three!*" Amy shouted in her effort to be heard above the roar of the raging water.

Suddenly, and as if they were one, their paddles entered the water and they began to battle with the current that seemed determined to beat them. Slowly, their combined efforts showed signs of reward and the cumbersome craft yielded to their paddling as they began to make headway toward the island.

"*It's starting to work! We're gaining momentum!*" shouted Ty as he paddled with all his strength.

* * *

"What's that?" Amy shouted pointing downstream.

"That must be the giant boulder that THE OLD ONE told me about," Toolook said as he stared in the direction that Amy was pointing.

"What boulder?" Ty yelled while frantically looking down stream.

They weren't halfway across the river and there it was: a giant boulder that split the river in two. They were rocketing towards the boulder at an ever-increasing speed.

"Jiminy-Willie-Peppers, we're going to crash," howled Parker as he viewed the oncoming boulder.

"Hang on!" Amy yelled.

"The current should take us around the boulder. When we get past it, paddle frantically so that we can get into the eddy that is created behind it, then we will be able to have a rest," shouted Toolook above the roar.

As they passed the boulder Amy shouted, *"now paddle with all your might!"*

The cumbersome craft yielded to the paddling and slipped gently into the quiet waters behind the boulder.

"If you knew this boulder was here why didn't you tell us?" Ty wanted to know.

"THE OLD ONE told me there was a boulder in the middle of the river and if we got to it we could rest in

its eddy. I didn't know if we would make it to the island before we got to this boulder or not. I didn't think it was necessary to mention it before," Toolook muttered as he shrugged his shoulders.

"Well, I think you should have mentioned it," howled an exhausted Ty.

"Well I for one could use the rest. I'm beat," said Parker as he laid his paddle down.

"After what we've been through we could all use a rest! We're still not even half way across the river," exclaimed Amy as she tried to catch her breath.

"What else did THE OLD ONE tell you that you haven't told us?" Ty demanded to know.

The group enjoyed the rest from the strenuous paddling they had been doing. The river's raging current was just about all they could handle.

"THE OLD ONE told me the river parts downstream from this big boulder and that half the river goes over a waterfall and the other half becomes a gently flowing stream that can be easily navigated by an Umiak. If we haven't reached the island before that point we will have no trouble reaching it once we hit the calm waters. But we have to make sure we don't go over the falls. There is no way back if we go over the falls," advised Toolook.

"Jiminy-Willie-Peppers!" exclaimed Parker as he stared at Toolook in disbelief.

"*This sounds like a fine mess you've gotten us into,*" Ty retorted.

"*Ty, watch your manners - we're all in this together,*" Amy scolded her brother.

Parker sat and listened to the banter. What had started out to be an enjoyable adventure had suddenly turned into a lot of work, and dangerous work at that. They rested in the Umiak as it gently floated in the eddy that the giant boulder created and tried to regain the energy they spent getting this far.

"*Do you think the rest of the way will be as hard as this part has been?*" asked Parker as he looked at the group.

"*It's not going to get any easier, you can bet on that; we're not even half way across,*" Ty observed with little enthusiasm as he looked across the expanse of river yet to be crossed.

"*Well, we're not going to get there by sitting here,*" Amy moaned while picking up her paddle.

"*You're right Amy, we must go,*" said Toolook.

"*Ready? All together now! Let's get our paddling synchronized before we hit the fast water. One-two-three!*" Amy yelled as the paddles swung into action and the cumbersome craft inched towards the fast water.

* * *

The craft spun crazily as soon as it hit the fast water and the crew was again paddling with all their might to gain some headway and try to reach the far shore as soon as possible. They had seen enough of this river and wanted no further part of it.

"What's that noise?" yelled Amy looking frantically around.

They could hear the thunderous roar and though the rapids were noisy, they were nothing compared to the roar that now filled their ears. They frantically searched the horizon to locate the source of the roar, but they could see nothing, and the thunderous roar continued to increase in volume.

"Jiminy-Willie-Peppers, it-it's got to be the waterfall that Toolook told us about. Nothing else could make that kind of noise," Parker whispered with a shaky voice and fear in his eyes.

Try as they might the group couldn't see the falls. They could hear them and the roar alone made it feel like they were on top of them.

"We've got to paddle harder; we can't go over the falls!" Amy screamed at the group, trying to be heard above the deafening roar.

They were consumed by fear and dug deep to find the inner strength to paddle harder. That unknown quality that sets achievers apart from the rest was being severely tested today. They knew what they had to do and they were doing everything in their power to do it. They paddled like they were possessed and, thankfully, the Umiak slowly responded to their efforts.

"What's that?" Amy yelled as she pointed to a rock face that was growing larger by the second.

"It's the divide we've got to get to the right of it, to the left are the falls!" Toolook bellowed.

"Paddle harder!" screamed Amy as her paddle dug deep into the rushing waters.

Amy, her brothers, and Toolook put their heads down and paddled as hard as they could. They all gave a sigh of relief as the Umiak slipped past the rock divide and ceased its crazy gyrations and settled into a nice easy drift on the calm waters.

"Jiminy-Willie-Peppers, did you see the water rushing over the falls?" Parker wailed as he looked at Ty.

"Boy I'm glad that's over, I never want to come that close to a waterfall again," sighed Ty while laying down his paddle.

"We're not on the island yet. Keep paddling and we'll have a rest when we reach shore," Amy yelled.

With weary arms, the foursome returned their blades to the river and paddled towards the island. The paddling was easy in the tranquil waters and they made good headway. Eventually the

Umiak was at last beached on the shore.

*   *   *

With the Umiak safely on shore, the group sprawled on the gravel to get some much needed rest.

"We'll rest awhile and then we've got some more work to do before we go to the tents," Amy advised the group.

"What have we got to do now?" Ty wanted to know.

"Well, take a look around you - our Umiak is here with us but we can't make the other shore from here, we've got to take the Umiak up the island before we launch it again," Amy said.

"I was afraid you were going to say something like that," Ty groaned.

"We'll do it Amy," Parker quipped as he smiled at his sister.

"Yes, we'll have to do that or we'll never get back," stated Toolook.

"Boy we're really in a fine mess now, aren't we? Maybe there's another Umiak that we can use up the

61

island and then we won't have to carry this one," Ty pleaded, looking at Amy.

"I wouldn't get my hopes up on that thought, nothing has come easy yet," Amy said to Ty.

"It shouldn't be that bad; with two of us on each side, we should be able to carry it up the shore," Parker offered to all who would listen.

"It's not that heavy, it's just awkward to carry but we'll manage," Amy said.

"We must hurry. We still have lots to do," Toolook stated as he got up from his rest.

"Yes, we have lots to do," repeated Amy as she got up. *"Parker and I will take this side of the Umiak. Ty, you and Toolook can take the other side. When our arms get tired we can change sides."*

Silently the foursome took their positions and started the long trek up the shore of the island, carrying the Umiak. They had been traveling together for so long that they didn't even have to speak when their arms tired; they just laid the Umiak down, changed sides and continued their trek northward. Talking would just take more of their precious energy and they had much to do before they saw the last of this island. Onward they walked as the gravel crunched beneath their feet. They changed sides many times and passed the tents of the never-ending feast. Still they walked north towards the end of the island. To ensure they had a chance of reaching the mainland, they had to start at the north end of the island. They had to reach the mainland before they encountered the giant boulder because there would not be enough river left for them to reach the shore if they had to rest at the boulder. A trip over the falls that they had barely missed was not a thought that they wanted to entertain - it would have been a trip to oblivion, and one with no return.

"I think I can see the end of the island," Parker shouted excitedly as he looked northward.

"You're right, it is the end. See how the river divides!" Amy observed while looking up the shore. The joy they felt in realizing that the end of carrying the awkward Umiak was near, brought a surge of energy to all of them. The newfound strength put a bounce in their step and they quickly reached the end of the island. They secured the Umiak so that it would remain where they could easily reach it - they were anticipating a hasty retreat from the island.

"Boy, I'm glad that part of the trip is over, I just wish we were on the other side of this river now and heading home," Ty muttered to his travel companions.

chapter vi

tents of the netherworld

When they left the Umiak and started toward the tents of the never-ending feast, they felt that something was amiss. The camaraderie that they should have came across was missing. There was no laughing and no signs of good times. Something was wrong on the island - a sense of foreboding filled the air.

"*Why do we not hear laughter and the usual sounds that accompany a feast?*" Amy asked Toolook.

"*I do not know. I fear something is not right on the island,*" replied Toolook.

"*I'll bet it's because the stolen soul is here!*" Parker remarked.

"*Yeah, it's not dead and it shouldn't be here,*" replied Ty.

"*That's right, it hasn't earned its spot in the tent of the never-ending feast. The other souls know this and it is upsetting them,*" stated Toolook.

"*Why do the dead souls keep the soul of their relative here, if it's not supposed to be here?*" Amy inquired.

"*I do not know, perhaps one of the souls will tell us why when we find their tent,*" replied Toolook.

They continued to talk as they neared the closest tent.

"*Check this tent and see if the stolen soul is here,*" Parker excitedly shouted as he looked at Toolook.

Toolook pulled back the tent flap and revealed the occupants enjoying the never- ending feast; they never looked up from eating.

"*This is not the tent that we seek!*" declared Toolook as he dropped the tent flap and stepped away.

The group got the same response from the second and third tents that they checked.

"How many more tents do we have to check before we get the right one?" Ty asked, looking at Toolook.

"As many as it takes to find the stolen soul," Amy replied to her brother.

The tents all looked the same: animal hides covered the framework of bones and driftwood that made up the structure of the tent. A smoke hole could be seen in the roof and a faint whiff of smoke was visible, lazily rising from the hole. Rocks ringed the tent base and held the animal skins in place.

When Toolook lifted the flap of the fourth tent, the group immediately noticed a difference. Although the other tents had been quiet, the dead souls had been enjoying the never-ending feast. In this tent, however, all the dead souls, with one exception, did not appear to be enjoying the never-ending feast and were huddled against one wall.

"This is the tent, isn't it Toolook?" Parker blurted out upon seeing the dead souls against the wall.

"I don't know," replied Toolook.

"Why is that one soul sitting by himself?" inquired Amy.

"Jiminy-Willie-Peppers this is getting spooky," cried Parker.

"*Who is the Elder? Who speaks for this tent?*" Toolook demanded as he stuck his head inside the tent.

"*I am the Elder and I speak for this tent. Who are you?*" asked the dead soul who had been sitting by himself. He got up and turned to face Toolook and the kids.

"*I am Toolook, the shaman, and these Kabloonas are assisting me on my quest to recover a stolen soul,*" replied Toolook as he faced the dead soul.

"*Why have you come here, there is nothing for you.*" the Elder stated.

"*We believe a stolen soul is here,*" Toolook informed the Elder.

"*Only our relatives are here. There is no one who doesn't belong,*" the Elder replied.

"*Why are the souls over against that wall and not sitting with you enjoying the never-ending feast?*" inquired Toolook.

"*They are protecting a relative's soul,*" answered the Elder.

"*Why does the relative's soul need protection?*" asked Toolook.

"*It doesn't want to stay,*" said the Elder.

"*How did the soul come to be here?*" asked Toolook.

"*The Keeper caught him wandering and now he has to stay,*" declared the Elder.

"*His journey is not yet finished on earth. His family is sad, his wife has no meat for the pot because she has lost her hunter. His kids are unhappy and cry because their dad doesn't darken their doorway anymore,*" Toolook told the Elder.

"*He will stay! Come share our feast and then you will have to leave,*" the Elder said to Toolook and the kids.

"*I will speak to the Keeper,*" Toolook told the Elder.

"*It is of no use, he will not talk to you about this soul. He-will-stay!*" the Elder flatly stated.

"*What are we going to do now? It looks like we've made this trip for nothing.*" Ty stated as he threw his hands up in the air.

"*Well, we'll have to decide what we're going to do; it doesn't sound like they're going to let us take the soul back to its owner. What do you want us to do now, Toolook?*" Amy asked.

"*Jiminy-Willie-Peppers, we better decide quick because we've got a long journey back and if that dog eats the other fish before we get to him, we'll be staying here forever whether we want to or not.*" As Parker spoke, he looked from one person to the next, his eyes as big as saucers.

Toolook and the kids moved to one side of the tent to discuss their next course of action. They would have to do something as it seemed the dead souls were not going to co-operate. The journey had been long and perilous and they could not afford to give up just yet. They would need a plan.

"*Did THE OLD ONE say anything to you about what to do if the dead souls wouldn't release the stolen soul?*" Amy asked Toolook.

"*THE OLD ONE did say that the dead souls might not want to let the stolen soul go,*" Toolook admitted.

"*Well, what did he tell you to do?*" Ty demanded.

"*THE OLD ONE said we might have to fight the dead souls to free the stolen soul,*" Toolook told the kids as they stared at him in shocked silence.

"*Jiminy-Willie-Peppers,*" cried Parker as he stared at Toolook.

"*What! Fight them? Are you crazy? Look how many of them there are - we can't fight them!*" exclaimed Ty, not believing what he was hearing.

"*Ty, don't get excited,*" Amy cautioned her brother.

"*I don't like the sounds of this,*" Parker said as he shook his head and looked across the tent at the

70

large number of dead souls he could soon be fighting.

"How did we ever get into this mess?" Ty wailed as he looked at Amy.

"What else did THE OLD ONE tell you Toolook?" Amy asked.

"He said the Kabloonas could distract the dead souls by fighting them and then I could grab the stolen soul during the confusion when no one was looking," Toolook told the kids.

"That's just great, we're doing the fighting and he's just going to grab the stolen soul. Why can't you do the fighting?" Ty asked Toolook.

"Ty, remember we're all in this together. If THE OLD ONE told Toolook that we should do the fighting and he should grab the soul, there's probably a good reason for it," Amy warned Ty.

"There are a lot more of them than there are of us Amy," Parker observed.

"I know there are Parker, we just have to come up with a plan that will work," Amy replied.

Parker had been observing the dead souls from across the tent and he noticed that quite a number of them were staring rather inquisitively at them. *"Why are those dead souls looking at us so funny?"* Parker asked as he looked at Toolook.

71

"*Most of the dead souls have never seen a Kabloona before,*" explained Toolook.

"*Then we're something of a novelty to them,*" said Amy.

"*Yes, you are. Come we must join the feast or they will become suspicious. It is an insult not to join the feast when you have been asked,*" added Toolook.

"*Well, I for one could have something to eat because I'm starving,*" stated Ty as he headed towards the Elder who was sitting alone and enjoying the never-ending feast.

"*I'm with you brother,*" Parker cried as he followed Ty to the feast circle.

"*The People like to wrestle, don't they?*" Amy asked Toolook.

"*Yes they do, why?*" Toolook said as he looked at Amy.

"*Well, I've got a plan and maybe we won't have to fight after all,*" Amy muttered.

The group took their places in the circle of the never-ending feast. Only the best cuts of meat are served at the never-ending feast and there is no end to the supply. Anyone who sits at the never-ending feast has earned his rewards honestly while toiling in the world before.

"*What is your plan?*" Ty asked Amy with doubt in his voice.

"Just a minute Ty. What else did THE OLD ONE tell you had to be done when you grab the stolen soul?" Amy asked Toolook.

"THE OLD ONE said I would have to swallow the stolen soul. After I have swallowed it I will not be able to open my mouth and I will have to plug my ears with my fingers to keep it from escaping," Toolook advised the kids.

"Here we go again! After we do the fighting we're going to have to do all the work paddling the boat back and everything because Toolook won't be able to use his hands. This is a fine mess we're in. What are we going to do now? Why can't we just grab it and run?" Ty howled as he looked at Toolook and then Amy.

"No, it will escape. THE OLD ONE said I must swallow it," Toolook informed Ty.

"I think I have a plan that will work. The People like to wrestle and it is one of their favorite pastimes when not working. When we've finished eating, Ty, you challenge one of the dead souls to a wrestling match. This should cause a distraction and maybe Toolook will be able to grab the stolen soul," Amy said to Ty.

"Jiminy-Willie-Peppers, do you think that will work Amy?" Parker wailed.

"Why me? Why do I have to challenge the dead soul?" Ty asked Amy.

"Would you rather I do it?" Amy asked Ty.

73

"Well no, I'll do it, but it better work," Ty said rather huffily to Amy.

Only the Elder sat in the feast circle with Toolook and the kids; the other dead souls warily watched from the other side of the tent. One could feel the tension in the tent. The kids eyed the dead souls with suspicion. What were the dead souls thinking? What would they do and what were they capable of doing? These questions raced through the kids' minds as they hungrily devoured their meals.

*   *   *

"I might as well get it over with," Ty remarked as he finished a tasty strip of seal meat and stood up.

"Jiminy-Willie-Peppers, which one are you going to challenge, Ty?" cried Parker. He could feel the tension in the room about to burst.

"I-I don't know, which one do you think I should challenge?" Ty asked, looking at the dead souls.

"Why don't you challenge the one on the far end; he looks to be about your size?" Amy suggested.

Ty walked nervously to the center of the tent, eying the potential opponent that Amy had pointed out to him. He quickly glanced over his right shoulder to assure himself that Amy, Parker and Toolook were where he left them and able to assist

74

him if he needed assistance. Once assured they were still behind him, his confidence bolstered and he faced his potential opponent to lay down the challenge.

The challenge was quickly accepted and before Ty realized what was happening, the wrestling match was on and he was rolling around on the ground with his surprising agile opponent. They tried to get each other in various holds and when that failed, they stood and tried to throw each other.

The other dead souls watched as the wrestling match progressed. It wasn't long before some of the dead souls got caught up in the excitement of the match and joined in the melee.

"Ty can't fight them all. There's too many. Come on, Parker, we've got to help him," Amy shouted as she flung herself into the free-for-all.

"Jiminy-Willie-Peppers I don't like this," Parker cried as he followed his sister and engaged the nearest dead soul.

When Amy and Parker joined the melee, the rest of the dead souls joined in and a gigantic struggle ensued. Souls were being flung in every direction but still more came.

"Is there no end to them? Where are they all coming from?" yelled Ty.

"Ty, watch your back," Parker howled as he hurled another soul to the corner of the tent.

"Be quick, Toolook!" Amy shouted. *"They are many and we are few, we cannot engage them forever."*

The battle raged back and forth with neither side accepting defeat. Toolook took advantage of the distraction and retrieved the stolen soul and swallowed it. In the excitement that ensued, it was easy to disengage from the melee because the dead souls were caught up in the moment and were wrestling each other - it had turned into a wild free for all! As quickly as the kids could, they disengaged from the wrestling match with the dead souls and headed for the river with Toolook in tow.

As soon as they left the tent with the stolen soul, the tension on the island abated; it was as if a cloud had been lifted. The sounds of laughter, burping and breaking wind, the sounds that generally accompany a great feast, could be heard across the island as the resident dead souls once again enjoyed the never-ending feast.

"I'm beat. I could use a rest after all that," Ty said to the group.

"We're all tired, Ty, and we'll have a rest at the Umiak before we cross the river but we can't afford to chance resting so close to the tent. Look at poor Toolook,

he can't even open his mouth and he has his fingers stuck in his ears," Amy laughed as she looked at Toolook.

"*Yeah, he looks funny,*" Parker piped in as he started to chuckle.

"*Hurry up, we've got a long way to go,*" Amy reminded her brothers.

chapter vii

the umiak awaits

The noise from the wrestling match diminished as Toolook and the kids left the tent behind and walked towards the shore. The Umiak, the only vessel that could provide them with safe passage across the river to the Road-Of-Shadows and home, was still awaiting them.

Upon reaching the Umiak, they all laid down on the shore for a much-deserved rest.

"Now I wish we hadn't left the Umiak so far from shore. It's going to be a lot more difficult to carry without Toolook's help," Ty observed as he lay looking at the cumbersome Umiak.

"We'll manage, don't worry Ty," Parker assured him.

"Do you think you can paddle the Umiak across the river without my help?" asked Toolook.

"Jiminy-Willie-Peppers, you can talk," a startled Parker squealed.

"Of course I can talk to you. We converse through our Inuas and don't use our mouths to speak," Toolook reminded him.

"That's right I forgot, you just startled me, you haven't said a word since you swallowed the stolen soul," Parker said.

"I think the three of us can do it if we all paddle together like we did before. Look how the river bends as it goes around the island; this is in our favour as we will be heading across and won't have the river bend away from us as it did when we came over," Amy screamed, trying to be heard above the roar of the mighty river.

"Don't worry, we've beat this river before and we'll beat the sucker again," Ty boasted as he felt his energy and self-assurance return.

chapter viii

the trip home

Amy, Ty and Parker carried the cumbersome Umiak to the edge of the river as Toolook trailed behind with his mouth shut and his fingers still stuck in his ears.

"*Boy, you sure look funny with your fingers stuck in your ears,*" Parker said to Toolook as he again began to laugh.

"*You'd look just as funny as Toolook if you were doing the same thing,*" Amy chided Parker.

"*Why don't you save your strength, we're going to need it to cross this river,*" Ty told Parker.

"*Toolook, when you get in the boat, sit in the middle. Ty can paddle from the right side and Parker and I will paddle from the left side. That should keep us pretty well balanced - we don't want to get tipped in this river,*" Amy said.

The kids pushed the Umiak into the water and held it while Toolook took his place in the middle. The stern of the Umiak still rested on the shore.

"*Ok Ty, you and Parker get in and take your positions and I will push us off. As soon as I yell, start paddling - we're not going to have any room for error! Remember, we've got to be on the other shore before we pass the giant boulder we rested behind or we'll go over the falls,*" Amy yelled as she shoved the Umiak off the shore and jumped in.

Immediately the current took hold of the Umiak and they found themselves once again spinning out of control and careening around like drunken sailors.

"*Jiminy-Willie-Peppers, we're out of control again,*" screamed Parker above the roar of the river.

"*Together, we have to paddle together! Ready, one-two-three!*" yelled Amy to her brothers.

With the kids paddling in unison, the Umiak began to yield and slowly edged further away from the shore.

"I wish Toolook could help us, this current is strong," Ty muttered.

"I wish he could too, however you know he can't because the stolen soul will escape if he does," Amy yelled to Ty.

"Save your breath and paddle hard!" cried Parker. *"We're in a race against this river that we must win!"*

The kids put their heads down and concentrated on their paddling. They never looked up because they knew that without Toolook paddling, they would need all the strength they could muster to complete this task successfully. No one relished the thought of going over the falls into oblivion. They paddled and their arms began to ache and still they paddled. They were being driven by the kind of power that could only come from fear.

Toolook sat in the center of the Umiak and stared straight ahead, oblivious to the spinning and crazy gyrations of the Umiak.

"I can see the other shore," yelled Toolook as he stared straight ahead.

"Can you see the giant boulder yet?" Amy cried.

"No, I cannot see it, it must be farther down stream," answered Toolook.

"Are we half way across yet?" Ty howled.

"I don't know, I can't see the shore we left, maybe we are, because I can see the other shore," Toolook replied to Ty.

"Save your breath and paddle," yelled Parker. Hearing that Toolook could see the shore gave the kids a burst of energy and they dug their paddles into the raging river with renewed vigor. On they paddled as the clumsy Umiak lurched and tossed on its journey across the river. Would this trip ever end? Not only were the kids arms aching from paddling, now their shoulders ached and it was only the fear of the falls that drove them on.

"I can see the giant boulder," shouted Toolook above the roar of the river.

"Where is it?" screamed Amy.

"I can only see the top of it; it's a long way downstream yet. I think we are past it and almost to the other shore," Toolook screamed above the raging river.

The news about the giant boulder was welcome and it lifted the paddlers' spirits. Their arms and shoulders ached and the paddles felt like they weighed a ton, but they paddled on, never letting up for a second. With their goal in sight, they could not afford to lose any ground. The distant shore began to grow larger, as did the giant boulder.

"It looks like we will hit the shore across from the giant boulder if we keep going the way we're going," Toolook yelled to the kids.

"As long as we don't go past the giant boulder and over the falls, I don't care where we land on shore," Ty quipped.

The kids' furious paddling produced the desired results and they soon felt the bottom of the Umiak scraping the river bottom. Amy jumped out of the Umiak and, grasping the gunwale, quickly pulled the Umiak up on shore. Ty and Parker fell out of the Umiak and lay on the shore gasping for breath, exhausted. After Toolook got out of the Umiak, Amy pulled it on shore and lay down with the boys to catch her breath. The kids couldn't remember when they had been so exhausted. Toolook sat on the shore while the kids lay on the rocks recovering from their ordeal.

"It will be good to get on the Road-Of-Shadows and get home," Ty said as he sat up.

"Yes it will, but we have one chore to do before we can continue our trip," Amy advised the group.

"What - what else do we have to do?" Ty asked looking at Amy as if he couldn't believe his ears.

"We have to return the Umiak, don't we?" Parker muttered in a dejected voice.

"That's right little brother, it has to be returned incase the next visitor requires it," Amy flatly stated.

"Oh no!" cried Ty.

"Amy is right!" Toolook added. *"THE OLD ONE said we have to leave things as we found them in the netherworld."*

"Yes, and it's going to be harder this time as there are only the three of us to carry it," Amy informed her brothers.

"Let's get it over with then," Ty whispered as he got up and took hold of the gunwale of the Umiak.

Silently the little group started the trip up the shore carrying the Umiak with Toolook following behind. They changed sides many times during the trip because they were a lot more tired now than they had been and on top of it all, they had one less person carrying the Umiak. When they reached the little backwater where they had found the Umiak, the group felt like a great burden had been lifted from their shoulders. And, indeed, a great burden had been lifted. With the Umiak again secured on the shore of the backwater, the little group headed out for the Road-Of-Shadows.

* * *

Free of the cumbersome Umiak, the kids and Toolook reached the Road-Of-Shadows in no time at all. As soon as they did, however, they found that the shadows were everywhere.

"*Jiminy-Willie-Peppers those shadows still give me the creeps,*" Parker howled as he ducked another shadow.

"*Before we met you there were shadows like these that appeared and disappeared in front of us. They scared us. What were they doing?*" Amy questioned Toolook.

"*They would have been shadows from the Road-Of-Shadows coming to scare you away from traveling the road,*" Toolook told the group.

"*Why would they do that?*" Amy inquired.

"*If you can be scared away from traveling the road you will not upset the tranquility of the netherworld,*" Toolook advised the kids.

"*If that's what they were trying to do, it didn't work,*" Ty boasted with a note of bravado sounding in his voice.

The group walked in silence until they saw the Keeper standing in the middle of the road.

"*Do you think the Keeper will give us any trouble when we try to pass?*" Amy asked Toolook.

"I don't know, we'll see when we get closer," replied Toolook.

When the group neared the Keeper he walked to the side of the road and watched as the group passed. The Keeper did not speak a word or even acknowledge the group.

"Well, I guess that answers that question. He didn't even acknowledge us," Parker said to no one in particular.

The group was tired from their ordeal and continued in silence along the Road-Of-Shadows. The shadows still tormented them; they coped with them by ducking and weaving when the shadows passed close. The back of the huge dog loomed large in the center of the road as he lay with his back to the group, forever guarding the road.

"I hope the dog hasn't eaten all the fish, I don't want to fight him to get past," Ty cried as he peered ahead at the dog.

"Well, he's busy chewing on something. You can see his head moving," observed Parker.

"It's the fish! Look you can see the tail of it on the road. We're in time - he hasn't finished eating yet," Amy yelled.

The group quickly came up to the dog and gave a sigh of relief as they passed him without incident. The dog was busily eating the second fish they had caught. Toolook and the kids continued up the road and past the house of the old woman who guards the gateway to the netherworld. Her door was closed and they did not stop to knock. Onward the group traveled - they could feel the end of their journey was near.

"How old is THE OLD ONE?" Amy asked Toolook.

"I do not know, he was THE OLD ONE when I was a young man," replied Toolook.

"About how old would that make him?" asked Amy.

"What does it matter? How old are the mountains, how old are the rivers, how old is the ocean? It does not matter. When they are needed they are there. Age is only the time that has passed," Toolook informed her.

"You won't tell us will you?" Amy inquired.

"I don't know, he has always been here," Toolook replied.

"He must be really old if Toolook calls him an old man for Toolook is an old man himself," Ty observed.

"Not necessarily. You're thirteen and to you, a person who is twenty is an old person," Amy reminded him.

"That's right, all things are relevant," Parker

added, not wanting to be left out of the conversation.

"Well I think THE OLD ONE is older than any of us thinks," Amy told the group.

"We'll probably never know," sighed Parker.

The talking helped them forget how tired they were and the miles quickly passed as they continued on their homeward journey.

*   *   *

The villagers were silent when the group returned. The People were still sitting in a circle around the sick Inuit just as they had been when the journey began. The sick man lay motionless on his bed of animal skins and had not moved. Toolook's assistant kept beating the drum. It echoed in the air: Boom-Boom-Boom.

The kids noticed that one thing was different, however, for in the circle now sat Kadluk, THE OLD ONE.

"Kadluk!" the kids yelled in unison upon seeing their friend.

"Yes, it is I," replied Kadluk.

As soon as their spirits returned to their bodies, they untied each other. Toolook went to the sick Inuit and returned his stolen soul. He was happy to be able to open his mouth and take his fingers from his ears. The sick Inuit was immediately well and rose from his sick bed. The People gave thanks because a good hunter had been returned to them. A feast was in order and the villagers got ready to celebrate.

"You will stay for the feast," Toolook pleaded with THE OLD ONE and the kids.

"No, it is time to go," stated THE OLD ONE.

"Then, I, Toolook, will sing the praises of the young Kabloonas at the feast," Toolook informed THE OLD ONE and the kids.

"Kadluk, you won't believe the trip we've been on," Amy shrieked.

"There will be time for talking later, now we must go," Kadluk flatly stated.

The last thing Amy remembered was Kadluk saying they had to go as her head hit the pillow and she fell asleep.

The kids were happy they could be of service to the old shaman and although the odyssey had been fraught with danger, they felt exhilarated by the events that had taken place.

* * * The end * * *

GLOSSARY

Inua – (inh'oo ah) n, the spiritual occupants, or spirit helpers, that reside in all living or inanimate things

Inuit – (inh' oo it) n, the people

Inyusuq – (personal souls) n, the powerful forces that reside within individuals and served as the source of good health, stamina, will power, and energy-all the elements that gave a person life. To drive out evil spirits healthy friends and relatives would give their Inyusuq to a sick person.

Kabloona – n, white man

Kayak – n, an Inuit one-man canoe-like boat consisting of a frame covered with animal skins

Shaman – (Sham-man) n, 1 a priest of shamanism. 2 a medicine man or witch doctor of a similar religion. (were thought to have special abilities in relating to the supernatural powers)

Shamanism – (sham-man-iz-zum) n, a religion of northern Asia, based on a belief in good and evil spirits who can be influenced or controlled only by the shamans. shamanist n, adj.

Tarrak – a dark, angry, enraged and malicious spirit. If relatives did not adhere to certain taboos after a person's death, the dead person's soul became enraged and malicious. This dark angry spirit was known to some Inuit as a personal shade or tarrak.

Umiak – (oo-mee-ak) n, a large open boat made of stretched skins, used by the Inuit (commonly called woman's boat)

The Author

Lawrence was born and raised in Alberta. 37 years of his adult life was spent serving in the Canadian Armed Forces and the Royal Canadian Mounted Police. The author draws on 10 years of living in the Yukon and the Northwest Territories for the inspiration for his stories. Retirement finds him again in Alberta where he presently lives with his wife Judith. They have 2 children and 6 grandchildren.

The Illustrator

Rob Adams, son of Lawrence Adams; when he is not working on his fathers illustrations, can be found working on game designs. Trained in Visual Communication, Rob currently works in the field of video games, juggling roles of a producer and game designer. Rob has had first hand experience of living and visiting many of the places described in the Trapps Family Adventure books.

GIVE A "**LAWRENCE E.R. ADAMS**" BOOK TO A FRIEND

Trapps Publishing
P.O. Box 212
Irricana, AB T0M 1B0
E-mail: trapps@efirehose.net

Send to:

Name:_____

Street:_____

City:_____

Province/   Postal/

State:_____Zip Code_____

Please Send:

"THE OLD ONE"   ____   X @ $9.95 =_____
"THE AMULET"   ____   X @ $9.95 =_____
"THE STOLEN SOUL"   ____   X @ $9.95 =_____

Shipping and handling for first book @ $4.00
plus $1.00 each additional Book   =_____
                                5% GST =_____
                    Total amount enclosed: _____

Make cheque or money order payable to:
TRAPPS PUBLISHING
Price subject to change without prior notice.
ORDERS OUTSIDE OF CANADA must be paid in U.S.
funds by cheque or money order drawn on U.S. or Canadian
Bank.
Sorry no C.O.D.'s.

Other books by Lawrence E.R. Adams.

the old one
the amulet

Watch for future books by Lawrence Adams as the Trapps Family Adventures continue to explore the mysteries of the north.

the creator
the mine
the famine
who walks on my land
who swims in my waters
who flies in my skies
the spirit of marble island
the search for the red diamond
the little people
the rescue

Join Amy, Ty and Parker as they continue to seek answers to life's adventures on the frozen tundra.